Wizard and Wart in TROUBLE

story by Janice Lee Smith
pictures by Paul Meisel

HarperCollins*Publishers*

To Kristen and Christopher Lee
with love, Great Aunt Janice

For Tom, Rolla, Maddy and Jake
—P.M.

HarperCollins®, 🖋®, and I Can Read Book®
are trademarks of HarperCollins Publishers Inc.

Wizard and Wart in Trouble
Copyright © 1998 by Janice Lee Smith
Illustrations copyright © 1998 by Paul Meisel
Printed in the U.S.A. All rights reserved.

Library of Congress Cataloging-in-Publication Data
Smith, Janice Lee, 1949–
    Wizard and Wart in trouble / story by Janice Lee Smith ; pictures by Paul Meisel.
        p.   cm. — (An I can read book)
Summary: Although they misunderstand when Zounds says that trouble is coming, Wizard and
his dog Wart manage to handle the spark ants, flood, and cold weather that ensue.
    ISBN 0-06-027761-0. — ISBN 0-06-027762-9 (lib. bdg.)
    [1. Wizards—Fiction.   2. Magic—Fiction.   3. Animals—Fiction.]   I. Meisel, Paul, ill.
II. Title.   III. Series.
PZ7.S6499Wk   1998   97-34353
[E]—dc21   CIP
                                                                                            AC

2   3   4   5   6   7   8   9   10
❖

Visit us on the World Wide Web!
http://www.harperchildrens.com

CONTENTS

Chapter One

"Trouble," said Zounds.

"I didn't know Zounds can talk,"
Wart said.

"He only talks

when he has something to say,"

said Wizard.

"Trouble is coming!" said Zounds.

"What kind of trouble?"

Wart asked.

"Big trouble!" said Zounds.

"We need to be ready," Wizard said.

"I will clean my magic closet,

in case the trouble is tricky."

"I will hide my bones," Wart said,

"in case the trouble is hungry."

Wart tried out his karate chops.

"Trouble might be bad guys,"

he said.

Wart tried out his screams.

"Trouble might be monsters,"

he said.

Wizard cleaned out

the pockets of his magic cloak.

He found old movie tickets

and some gum.

Wart hid the gum with his bones.

"What do we do now?" Wart asked.

"We are as ready as we can be,"

Wizard said.

"Now we wait for trouble to come."

Chapter Two

Wizard and Wart waited.

A rabbit ran past.

"Save yourselves!" he yelled.

Wizard looked down the road.

"Big trouble!" he said.

"It's spark ants.

They march into your house

and set fire to everything."

"With magic?" Wart asked.

"With matches," Wizard said.

Clomp. Clomp. Clomp.

The ants marched up to the door.

"They are very loud ants,"

said Wart.

"They arc wearing boots,"

Wizard told him.

The lead ant was named Bob.

"Out of the way!" he yelled.

"Watch out, fur face.

I'll make you a hot dog!"

"Never dance with ants

in your pants," Wizard sang.

18

Poof!

The ants turned into butterflies.

"I have never seen a butterfly

wearing boots before," said Wart.

"In three days

I'll make you ants again,"

Wizard said.

"But only if you promise

to behave."

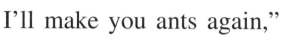

"You are no fun," Bob said.

"That takes care of trouble,"

Wizard told Wart.

"I hope you are happy now,"

Wart told Zounds.

Zounds didn't look happy.

"Trouble is coming!" he said.

Chapter Three

"Zounds must be kidding,"
Wart said.

"There cannot be more trouble!"

"Zounds never kids," said Wizard.

The rabbit ran by.

"Save yourselves all over again!"

he yelled.

"The river is flooding!" Wart cried.

Cows floated past.

Chickens swam the breast stroke.

"I can dog-paddle," said Wart,

"but I cannot swim!"

Wizard hocused and pocused.

"Floods and mud to leaf and bud!"

he sang.

Then Wizard sneezed.

Poof!

The water became whipped cream.

"Yum!" said Wart.

"Can you take out the cows

and the chickens?"

"Wrong spell," said Wizard.

He sang it again without sneezing.

Flowers grew

where the whipped cream had been.

"Wow!" said Bob.

"Follow me, guys."

"Darn," said Wart.

"I really love whipped cream."

"Trouble is coming!" said Zounds.

Chapter Four

"We have already had trouble!"

Wart yelled.

"Trouble! Trouble! Trouble!"

said Zounds.

"You arc a birdbrain," Wart said.

The rabbit ran by.

"Save yourselves!" he cried.

"Save me too!"

"He is having a bad day,"
Wizard said.

"I am having a worse day,"
said Wart.

A freezing wind blew.

"It's an ice zing!" Wizard said.

"Brrrr," said Bob.

"Ouch!" Wart yelled.

"Something keeps pinching me!"

"Those are cold snaps,"

Wizard said,

"but they're not the worst part

of ice zings."

Pow!

"That's the worst part," said Wizard.

38

"From zingy to springy," he sang.

"Ring-a-ding-dingy!"

Poof!

A warm breeze blew.

Trees grew where the snow had been.

"It can't get better than this,"

Bob said.

Wizard added a rainbow.

"Great," said Bob.

"That's better!"

"That's showing off," said Wart.

"Big trouble is coming!" said Zounds.

Chapter Five

"I think we should just get rid

of the bird," Wart said.

"I don't see anything coming,"

Wizard said.

"And there's no rabbit running by."

There was a knock at the door.

"At least this trouble is polite,"
Wizard said.

"Open the door, Wart."

"What if it's ants with matches?"
asked Wart.

"What if it's something worse?"

"I'll fix whatever it is,"
Wizard said.

"Then you open the door,"
said Wart.

Wizard opened the door.

A pretty bird stood there.

"Here I am," she said.

She flew up to the rafters

and cuddled next to Zounds.

"Sweetie!" she said.

"Trouble is here!" Zounds cried.

Trouble snuggled closer to Zounds.

"I think our trouble is over

for today," Wizard said.

"Thank goodness," said Wart.

"But I think Zounds's trouble

is just starting."